Grief Hides in the Shadows

Brendan Rubin

For Zaidy.

By the same author:

Heart Burn (2024)

Contents

1. The Shadow 1

2. Learning to Remember 5

3. ALone(liness) 9

4. Kyle 15

5. REM 17

6. Lost Spirits 19

7. Papa Keith 21

8. elyK 27

9. Off Into the Wilderness 29

10. Librairie des Grands Esprits 33

11. You Know Better 37

12. The Cost of Pain 41

13. The Note 43

14. KkYyLlEe 47

15. Am I... Happy? 49

16. Pages & Plaisir 53

17. The Dilemma of Love   57

18. The Journey   61

19. A New Life   65

20. Goodbye, for Now   67

21. K...   69

Do Not Stand At My Grave And Weep   71

About the author   73

Chapter One
The Shadow

I'VE NAMED HIM KYLE. He follows me everywhere, mile after mile, into the shower, down dirt roads, into bed. He's been there since my father Keith passed away four months ago. An untimely death. Drunk driver hit him when he was going down Queen Mary road, at the trial no remorse did he show, my life since then, painfully slow.

Kyle isn't a person, as you may be thinking. Kyle is the shadow that follows me around, giving me no time to myself. My eyes with bags, joints feeling rusty, and my shelves getting dusty. He protects me from the outside world, prohibiting me from leaving my apartment. Kyle takes away my motivation, drains my social battery, and torments me with possible scenarios. Traps me in a world of pain, grief, and fear. Some may call it anxiety, depression, but no, it is my dear Kyle, keeping me safe, away from the evils of the world. If he had been there for my father, he would be able to pick up the phone, not decomposing down to the bone. If Kyle showed up two years ago, I would still have my wife Cynthia, and my kids, Parker and Liam[1] . That salty bitch took them in the trials, along with the house and my sanity.

But now, I have my sweetheart Kyle. Enveloping me in darkness, stabbing me with pain, like a sword with such great sharpness. Spreading outwards, like the ever-growing universe, consuming everything in his path. A spectacle to observe, to be a part of.

***

To die,

Means to stop living.

It's true to an extent. Being alive and living your life are vastly different. Since my dad took his last breath, I've just been alive. Going through the motions, numb to my emotions, drowning out the world with alcoholic potions. Although I haven't brought myself to do much work over the past few months, my boss has been accommodating enough. We've come to an agreement, where I do work once a week, and he pays me for the hours I do online. It covers the rent, and I sharpen my skills in computer programming. He needs me to keep the website running for the company's musicians. They need to access our resources and contact information. I don't often hear their mu-

---

1. Seven and five years old, respectively.

sic on the radio station, keeping myself in isolation, enjoying when I drink and get that carefree sensation.

I look around my 2.5 apartment. I could downsize. I don't see my couch anymore, I haven't used my kitchen in months, not even sure if the stove still turns on. Clothes cover the floors, pizza boxes stacked as tall as my doors, scattered empty bottles of Coors, what have I done? Where have I been? Kyle is hugging me. Pulling me towards my bed, through my months-worth piles of laundry, under my covers.

It's time to sleep this off, Callum, I tell myself. Nothing could hurt me while I sleep. I'll worry about the mess when I wake up. Maybe.

Chapter Two
Learning to Remember

I'VE BEEN TOSSING AND turning all night. I'm still avoiding the fact that my father's gone. I text him, call him, knowing damn well I won't get an answer, but I refuse to believe it. Kyle likes to remind me. He'll make me smell his cologne out of the blue, hear his name, reminisce on our times together.

Most recently, I was indulging in my endless scroll on social media, trying to distract myself. Kyle knocked me in the head, getting my attention, and pulled me into his trance.

2008. I was twenty-one years old and getting ready to move out of the house. Dad came up to me, glee in his eyes, telling me he got us a pass to go camping together. So excited to spend time with his son, be out in the wilderness under the sun, we'd be leaving tomorrow, the packing already done. That was such a fun weekend, never wanting it to end. We stayed by the water, the window in the tent looking out at the waves, he always did love the water, we fished for hours, talking, staying silent, listening to music, sitting in silence, whatever it was, it was peaceful, enjoying each other's presence, shhhh shhhh, hearing the reels come in, no fish in sight, no problem, it was still fun, sharing a laugh over our lack of skill catching fish, until Papa saw my fishing rod start to bend, the line extending like the daytime in the spring, he wrapped his arms around me, showing me how to bring it in, pull, reel it in boy, that's exactly it, and before we knew it I had a fish in my hands, pulling the hook out of it's mouth, smiles on both our faces.

Building up the bonfire, he was showing me all the tricks. To allow air to flow through, keep feeding the fire, the best ways to build it for an efficient cooking station. I always appreciated when he taught me something. He was always patient, caring, and clear with his words. No bullshit, but you could take your time. Exactly what I needed.

***

I loved traveling with him. Always seeking a new adventure, to put a smile on mine and mom's faces. Kyle reminds me to think about these times. Remember the fun trips, not the hard times. So that's what I do, lying alone in bed, no one to confide in, to talk to, other than my shadow companion, sinking into my bed, deeper than a canyon.

It's tough sometimes, though. That's because, to remember the good times, means to acknowledge they won't happen anymore. It reminds me that the stars don't shine as bright without him, jokes aren't as funny without his hand slapping his knee, life isn't as interesting without his random phone calls or ways he used to do things that purposefully pissed me off.

It is, for instance, fun to remember our road trips, our shared love of music, or our comical chemistry. The ways he would entertain a room with his jokes, or how he was always there for me. Anytime I needed a shoulder to cry on, to confide in, get advice or even get out of a tough situation.

My father and I shared a love for sports too. Unfortunately, both my mom and dad were incredibly competitive, and that was ultimately passed down to me. For several years, we led our hockey league in suspensions because of that urge and *need* to win. The Linsar boys watching from the side, father and kin, both committing sin.

Good times,

Fun times,

End of times.

Chapter Three
ALone(liness)

I SUDDENLY GET A nudge from Kyle. What time is it? What day is it? When was the last time I ate, went to the bathroom, interacted with others? I look outside and see the city around me moving, people getting from point A to point B, others walking around aimlessly. I remember those times. Times I would bring home presents for the kids, flowers for Cynthia, some chocolate bars to share with Dad. But now, what is there to do? No one to see, to support, to make happy.

I've been having discussions with Kyle lately. Or, I've been talking, and he's been surrounding me, not speaking, but stalking. There's been one theme that's returned a couple times. Am I lonely, or am I alone? Is there a difference, or even an importance to their discrepancies? I think we've finally come to a conclusion: yes, they're different. That took a couple weeks to figure out, but now I'm struggling to find the difference.

To be alone, means just that. You're alone, no one around. But I believe there's another sense to it, because although you're not alone physically in a mall, doesn't mean you're not *alone*. Sure, there's a crowd moving in and out of lanes, stores, but who's there with you in your thoughts? Struggling day in and day out, trying to help you, or do the simple thing of asking how you are. We're just secondary characters in everyone's life, which means no one's *with* anyone. So, I ask Kyle, *how is that any different from loneliness?*

Isn't loneliness exactly that? To be isolated and not have a way to outsource your thoughts? *Sigh*. Why does it all have to be so complicated? How I feel, and even finding the way to describe it? Thinking about the difficulty of that, sends me back to my thoughts about loneliness. A loop. Going in circles, driving me mad, running into corner after corner like it's plaid, being reminded of the times we had.

I find myself stuck on the smallest change of words. You could feel lonely, while not being alone, but you could also be alone but not feel lonely? Hm. Peculiar.

***

It's been a long time coming. It's time to clean the place up. No one's coming to visit, no women, no family, no landlord, I just can't deal with it much longer. It's nearly impossible now to even get to my bathroom. Not that I've needed it too much, but it's still a hassle. To put everything away, throw the boxes out, it makes me want to scream, shout, plan it out like a route, have to get it done, throw the boxes in the garbage, find where my washer and drier are, clean what I'll keep, discard the stained ones, it's draining, much of the stuff damp, as if it's been raining, the wash will do it good, make it new, I don't recognize much of the stuff, it's been a rough few months.

For the first time in a while, Kyle sits in the corner and keeps to himself. I think that's what's given me the motivation and the will to do this. Something tells me he wanted me to do this, that he's some type of neat freak, he was getting sick of the reek, needed it to be aired out. I don't blame him. To me, it's been a representation of my mind. For a while now. Dirtied, cluttered, filled with old, junky stuff. It's nice to let some light in, to see the floors once more. Maybe order some ingredients to cook – no – not yet. Maybe I'll order a salad, or at least something with vegetables in it. That sounds better, more doable.

***

Once I separate my laundry, bring my trash out to the curb for the first time in months, and soak in some sun, I'm faced with the rest of the cleaning. The floors, carpets, couches and bathroom. Mom used to show me how to do all that. Dad kind of just laid back and complained about it being dirty to get under her skin. It's not that he didn't know what to do or how to do it, I think he just did it poorly on purpose so it wasn't expected of him. Dad and his tricks. Always knew how to finesse a situation, to get his way. Not in a malicious way, just in small ways such as not having to clean, or going out to shop. He knew what he liked, didn't like and found his ways around them. So, mom had to dump her knowledge off on someone: me! Sure, thirteen-year-old me would have much preferred to be out with girls, going to the arcade, or playing ball with friends on a Sunday afternoon, but I had my whole life for that. This prepared me to clean my apartment that's been sent to the dump and back. I take a deep breath, get ready, and look for my cleaning supplies.

***

Scrub scrub, rub rub, wipe wipe, it's therapeutic in a way. My own therapy, except it's much cheaper, less scary and I don't have to share anything. I'm... content? No. I'm less lonely. I'm occupying myself, spending my time properly and not on video games, drugs, alcohol, irrelevant nonsense. I guess that's what life's about isn't it? Filling your life with things that help you reach your goals? Make sure you don't dig your hole deeper, use the dirt from holes you've dug to build the stepping stones to improve? I wonder what Kyle thinks, watching over me in the corner, making sure I use the right sprays for the windows, the counters. He must be proud. Or scared. When, or if, I don't need him any longer, will he be happy I'm getting better? Or upset he doesn't have a purpose? The flow of questions endless, like the opening scroll of Star Wars movies.

I find refuge in these questions. They help me think about something other than my issues. To find an answer is to fully engulf yourself in thought. There's no half-assing an answer. No skating around it like a dancer, leaving it until later. It keeps me going, maybe not away from the bottles, or the takeout, or the trash, but day-to-day. To wake up, and even just for a second be okay, the rest of the day, in my bed I lay.

But for now, all is clean. I can indulge,

Go to bed,

And breathe well.

Chapter Four

Kyle

Li-li-li-li lullaby watch that cry don't be shy rolled in bed like he's high darkness I will supply to protect to shield so he's safe safe from feelings he's concealed so many buried memories we've revealed I surround him make the light around dim he's improving showing improvements getting better I can tell he's started to shower again to eat properly our boy has even shaved his face thank the lord it was getting scraggly oh and smelly can't forget itchy it would tickle me make me laugh I promise I will leave one day but only when he's ready he needs me so I'll caress him hug him show him the warmth he needs in such trying times

I will be his protector

For as long as he needs

Then I will be gone

Liftoff.

Chapter Five
REM

I WAKE UP IN my king bed, roll over, hold my wife, soak in the morning sun, enjoying what I made in this life, two children, a wonderful job, a loving family, I'm happy, content, I look out the window and see a white butterfly, it reminds me to call my father, don't be shy, I know if he sees my number he won't deny, wouldn't even try, last night my buddies came over and we got high, I'm a little hungover, won't tell Pops he'll say I shouldn't hang with those guys, they're not for me, he's always said that, but I like them, they calm me, anyway, he picks up the phone, we chit-chat, it's always nice to hear his voice, we've had our ups and downs, but always make it up, watch some sports, some Jeopardy, enjoy some coffee, whatever it takes, I go downstairs to the kiddos, pour them each a bowl of Cheerios, give them the phone to say hi, Cynthia's in the shower, won't be able to say hi, it's okay, we've got to get ready for school, for work, for the day, take it in and push through, meetings and phone calls, nothing like a good sleep on the office couch, wife packed me a nice lunch, leftovers from last night, heat it up, see my coworkers get jealous, for my life they are jealous, how could they not be, life's perfect, we're all perfect, so perfect, why wouldn't we be perfect, *fuck*, I get home, park in the driveway, I feel the energy coming from the house, the happiness, the excitement, the dread, I go to open the door, it's locked, or blocked, I can't manage to swing it open, to see my kids, my wife, smell the home cooked meal, I'm stuck, out of my house I've been plucked, my worst fear, my deepest regret, I feel the chill surrounding me, shaking me, I become shackled and no longer free, I can't go on, that I could guarantee, the sun getting covered by a cold surge of clouds sweeping over it like a mother does to her child with his Transformers bedsheets, I curl up, unknowing of the future, close my eyes, and wait.

And I awake. Kyle standing over my bed, feeding me my dread, happiness exiting me like an open wound and I bled, until there was nothing left. It was nice while it lasted. It was nice to hear his voice, that he visited me in my dream.

But I don't feel him anymore.

He's gone.

I've lost him.

Chapter Six
Lost Spirits

How do I find you?

Where does your spirit go?

I'm looking for the smallest clue,

I'm lost, life starting to slow,

I need you, I miss you, I long for you,

Show yourself.

And come back,

To life, to light,

Tonight.

Chapter Seven
Papa Keith

We weren't always close. I didn't know much about him until I was grown, it was only then that his past was shown in a less serious tone yet it still rattled me to the bone. I didn't know my dad had been exiled. His family banished him, like it was the dark realm, when I learnt this I had been overwhelmed, not knowing how to react. How did my dad, the book shop owner, have such a dark past? No longer than twenty years did the relationship with his family last? It was abstract. Incomprehensible. The father I knew kept to himself, read in his free time, brought home flowers to my mom every week, calm as a butterfly, involved in his son's extracurriculars, never got mad, never even a raised voice, involved in schoolwork, encouraged whatever made me happy, was a huge audiophile, Jewish for the traditions, prioritized family over everything. Where could it have possibly gone wrong — especially with his *own* family? Embarrassment, if that even encompasses the entirety of the feeling, is what overcame me when I finally learnt this. My own father, to ask I didn't even bother, to know why I never met his side of his family. How much of an asshole do you have to be to not ask about your own kin, how big of a sin, the magnitude I couldn't even begin to think of.

***

Keith Joshua Linsar was the youngest of four children. His dad, Paul, an accountant, and his mom, Alma, a stay-at-home mother, birthed their fourth and final child on August 17, 1954, in Oakland, California. They were an ideal nuclear family, loving parents, four beautiful children, the need for money was never a burden, a large yard. My father grew up lucky. A wealthy family in a rather poor city, the other kids he would pity, give them his fruit snacks, be kind. That's something he naturally had: a massive sweet heart. He knew he'd have food to come home to, and they might not. He'd be glad to be hungry during the day if it meant his friends got to fend off the hunger just a bit longer.

School was always easy for my dad. An academic threat with no intention to keep it going, always the plan to become an author. He always loved reading, writing, imagining himself on the beach, completing novels, signing deals, going on release tours, having his groupies, adaptations to movies, when his moment came he knew he'd seize. He always believed words were immortal. They'd never go extinct. As motivated as he was to achieve his goals, his parents were never in support. They didn't see any money in it. He'd be a failure to them, living with them, depending on them. So, he lied. He said he'd given up on his dream, full ride scholarships he'd redeem, being the gifted child he had become.

He wrote under a pen name. Luke Speidth. His first book, The Science of Jew, was an immediate hit. He was an overnight success, books over the nation, any book store you'd walk into you'd see his name. Well accepted by some, it was wildly controversial for most. He delved into the world of literary fiction full force, telling the story of a world domination by Jews. How they took over the power in many sectors, CEOs, chairmen, directors, anything and everything that gleamed with potential. How they outsmarted many, destroyed the egos of the powerful, the rest of the world becoming lustful. His book releasing just months after the Munich massacre, it became the talking point for many people in power in the real world, exploring his words to determine whether the book had a place in the public. To see if it was safe for the Jewish population to have such an influential book readily available, to be used against them, to be used as an attack. This fuelled my father. It gave him strength to keep writing.

Being such a prominent work for scholars and readers alike, it was inevitable the book reached his father's desk. It was quickly a topic of discussion at the dinner table, which meant a very strong and unpopular reception while eating their mom's brisket.

***

A star takes a long time to form. It begins by gas colliding together, developing its own gravity. Over time, this gravity grows stronger and stronger, pulling in its own particles, along with attracting new gas. This takes millions of years. It's a slow process. This gas starts to collide into itself, creating tremendous heat and energy.

This was the exact reaction going on in my father's head when his family received the book so poorly. It fuelled something in him. A nuclear reaction of creativity occurring, creative fusion, ideas colliding with each other, developing massive ideas without end. At one point, Keith was writing for hours a day, without stopping, idea after idea, words flowing into his journal.

His next novel, he decided, would play on his own life. He would write about an author, who's parents didn't support his writing. *Brilliant*, he thought, *how many others would be able to relate to the story?* It wouldn't be as tough of a read as his debut, so it could be ingested by the broader public. He set his mind to it. Hours in the library, back hunched over, scribbling down his ideas, looking like a scrub. It didn't bother him. He learnt long ago to not worry about what others thought. It didn't hurt him that even his own two parents hated his dream and his first work of art, why should he care about a jabroni judging him for pursuing his passion in the local library? Ridiculous. He was too grown for that. So he wrote, words to the paper like a scream from the throat, hard words, long phrases, it came to him naturally.

He enjoyed the mundane aspects of the life. Sending it off to his editor, waiting for feedback, waiting for his release date, and seeing his second book climb to the top of the charts. Lightning does indeed strike twice, at least with talent of his caliber. However, things didn't go over so well at home. The book was clearly taking cheap shots at his parents, and he didn't try to hide it, make it subliminal. Paul and Alma got their hands on the book quickly, and life swiftly went south, screaming bouts, getting thrown out, setting a route for a new life. It all happened so quickly, he hardly had time to say farewell to his siblings, which didn't bother him too much. He was never too close to them. He bounced around from town to town, never settling down, until he met my mother. They met after he nearly ran her over in Boston. He was deep in thought, thinking about the novel he was writing, "The Big Bust," and he didn't see her crossing the street. They fell in love quickly, getting married after just a few months. The rest is history. Baby Callum was just a couple years away.

***

I'll never forgive myself for not knowing about his past earlier, but hindsight is 20/20. All I could do now is be grateful I was fortunate enough that he shared eventually. It's a story for the ages, and I have a dozen novels to read from my father, as he wrote until his passing. Always a success, but I never knew it. My mother is in charge of his estate and decided to not release posthumously. I agree. Let his legend be that. A work of the past, no need to milk his art. He released what he wanted to and didn't what he thought wasn't meant to be.

A wonderful author and an even better father.

Chapter Eight
elyK

Ru-ru-ru-ru run from the pain but then how could you explain describe how you made it out the rain it's important to feel to know how to make it out he often looks up to the sky he wonders why wonders why his father had to die but the pain he can't deny he has to leave to get up and go how else could I help him he can't stay in forever I shall push him to go he will start to know start to understand life has a certain glow and that there is a ground below and he could push himself up have the wonder and curiosity like a pup I believe in him I know I must push get him off his tush and go out

So I can know he's at peace

Let him off his leash

And flourish

Like the beautiful flower he is.

Chapter Nine
Off Into the Wilderness

SOMETIMES I DISGUISE THE truth, for myself, for comfort. I tell myself I'm okay, that I'm doing better. But it's not true. I'm stuck thinking of the days he was with me, full of glee. I get stuck in those ruts, an infinite loop. Feel like shit, tell myself I'm fine, indulge in some of life's intoxicants, and fall back into the loop. I need to break it.

Kyle's been leaving me hints on how I could do it. He'll let a nice breeze flow into my apartment, have my TV set to the nature channel, small hints. I think I'm ready. Ready but scared. I'm afraid of seeing things that remind me of my father, being sent down a rabbit hole with no way to hop out. But some things must be done. I can't stay on my couch scrolling endlessly. I can't live in the same 950 square feet of undecorated disgust for the rest of my life. I must venture out, learn to live once again.

***

I'm hyper-vigilant as I step out of the elevator. Ready for any and everything. A woman, around my age, gives me a smile as I go through the rotating doors and onto the street. I smell shawarma mixed with car exhausts. It puts a smile on my face. There's nothing better than the smell of a big city, the combination of pollutants and indulgences. I forget what it's like to be out, walk past others, give a faint smile, to look at passing cars and into the various buildings I pass. It's calming. The sounds of engines running, the faint bass coming from people playing their music, it's all simple but it feeds the soul like a warm home cooked meal. My shadow, Kyle, follows me, faintly, on the walls of the buildings I pass. Watching, protecting.

***

The echoes of the past bounce from wall to wall around me. The hairdresser I used to bring the kids to, the bar I'd drink at when I'd be forced to sleep on the couch, the movie theatre I had my first kiss in. It all stings to see. It all went by so quickly, I hadn't known to appreciate it when it was happening, that I took it for granted. I took the happiness for granted. The good memories, even the bad, not learning from them or enjoying as it happened. It flew by me at ultrasonic speed.

Cracks in the concrete, the sun shining down, my shins hurting, I'm walking with no destination in mind. Just to get out, it's a start. Exploring the wilderness of a concrete jungle, trying to escape my struggles, and the prison I created in my mind, in my own home, so the bustling streets I roam.

Following the crowds, thinking if I could have been a stronger man. To be the shepherd, not the sheep. Breathing in the air, I'm trying to keep pushing, to propel myself forward, upward, further. I decide to take a step to the side, lean on a storefront. I need to catch my breath. I've gotten quite out of shape these last few months. Breathing in and out, trying to meditate quickly like my father used to. He would always try new things, find new fads. We'd always make fun of him, tell him it's just a faze, he'd outgrow it shortly. This one though, lasted the longest. He liked to keep a level head, clear his mind. He would try to teach me but I'd just brush him off, find something else to do. As I got older, I realized it was a necessity. Life comes at you hard and sometimes you just need to decompress, get the weight off your chest like a bench press. In, out, focus on the breath, be mindful. Notice the smells, the sounds, focus on the exterior factors, push out the thoughts. My mind began to clear, like a venue when a concert ends. I decide to look into the store that I've been loitering outside of.

It's a book store.

I walk in.

Chapter Ten
Librairie des Grands Esprits

THE STORE OWNER GREETS me with a smile that could melt you down to your core. An independent bookstore, Librairie des Grands Esprits, The Bookstore of Great Minds. Her beauty catches me off guard. Curly brown hair, perfectly conforming to her face, springy and cute bangs that almost covered her gleaming brown eyes. She's tanned like she had never left her beach post in Florida, beautiful silver necklaces lining her neck to contrast her complexion. Her smile showed the cutest dimples, and could make me giggle like I was back on the playground with my pals. Shelley, I see on her name-tag. She offers me help with anything I needed, and I give back an awkward smile.

I go straight to the American Fiction section and try finding the area with the last names starting with S. They're all here. All of Luke Speidth's work. I take them all and bring them to the beautiful cashier. She rings me up and slips me an extra bookmark. As I get to the sidewalk, I look at what she gave me. Shelley Kirkstead, her number, and a little heart.

***

Smiling wide as a trench, a pep to my step, and finally a gleeful look in my eyes. Rather than holding me back, or stalking me, Kyle is pushing me forward. Propelling me back to my house to sit my ass down, text Shelley and start reading these books.

What a different day it was today! It was a good day. One of the best ones in a *long* time.

***

When I finally get back to my apartment complex – I didn't realize how long I had walked for – I walk up the stairs and unlock my door. Home sweet home. The moment I walk inside, I take out my phone and open my messages app quicker than I ever have before. I type Shelley's number in and I freeze. What do I text? What do I say? Is it too early to send a message, will I seem eager? I don't want to come across that way, don't want to scare her away so quickly. I also can't remember the last time I texted a romantic interest. My thoughts continue to race and I decide to put my phone away. I'll wait a bit. Craft up a text that'll work. I'm meticulous in that way. It'll be perfect, something that won't end in reject. Then again, she gave me her number. What could go wrong? I'll wait. It's best.

As I go to place my books on my coffee table, I bash my knee on my dinner table. Of course. I drop to the floor in pain, writhing on the ground. I take a few minutes to gather myself, there's not much more physical pain (for a man) than hitting an object when you weren't expecting it. Do we have it easy? Meh. I won't think about it. As I compose myself, I see my new books sprawled across the floor. As I pick them up, a little paper slips out of one of his books. It's a lined paper that you see in notebooks that you'd write in at school, folded up.

As I unfold the paper, my heart sinks. I stare at the paper as water begins to well up in my eyes, unable to read past the first word. I recognize the handwriting.

It's my dad's.

Chapter Eleven
You Know Better

"You know better, Callum."

Four words. That's all I ever needed to hear to know that I fucked up. My father was never big on punishments, he had too big of a heart. The very few times he actually punished me, he felt bad and rescinded his decision within a day, if not a couple hours. Rather, he was big on letting you know that you made a mistake. He'd let it sit with you, let his disappointment eat away at you, which is arguably much worse. You'd mess up, and boom. Four words and you're in your room beating yourself up over your mistakes, grilling yourself like a barbecue and a few steaks, understanding the stakes at hand.

So many instances of this come to memory, I was a difficult child. It wasn't that I was trying to upset anyone, I just never thought before acting. Impulsive and immature.

***

I was finishing up my earlier studies. I was set to move out for school, pursue computer science, make an honest living. Things decided to switch up on me. I started to experiment with drugs, go out with friends, the classics. Grades began to drop, I wasn't helping out around the house anymore, started to lie. My dad, living through what he had in his life, was prone to pick up on some of these signs. You can't out-bullshit a bullshitter. It's written in stone, in the stars.

He pulled me aside one day, away from my mom. He always did this when he had to have serious talks with me. He never wanted to stress her out. It wasn't that she couldn't handle it, it was just that he wanted to carry the weight on his shoulders, give her a break from any stress. He asked me if I had anything I wanted to share, if I needed help with anything. There was no judgment, as long as I was honest. What kind of teenager is honest with their parents? What kind of teenage boy is mentally aware and mature enough to acknowledge his mistakes? In my case, absolutely nothing. No Dad, I replied, why're you asking? And there it was. "You know better, Callum," and he left me in my room. What just happened? My frontal lobeless mind couldn't comprehend what had just occurred. It caused me to look inwards, something that had never been done before. Was I fucking up, making a fool of myself? What was I doing wrong, how could I fix it? Can I make amends or has it gone to shit? Rebuild the trust with my father or was it permanently split?

Keith was always great at making you look inwards, see how you could improve. That's what also made him such an incredible author. He had such an acute ability to express his thoughts onto paper, into words. His theory, was that if you're able to understand something as well as you know how to walk, being able to apply it to someone else is the same as doing it yourself. He applied it to everything he learnt. Expressing thoughts, lay out facts, show love.

Chapter Twelve
The Cost of Pain

Pain really isn't that cheap,

It takes from you,

It holds you back,

It doesn't let go.

Pain costs people their lives,

Pain doesn't let you think it through,

Pain doesn't give you time to look at facts,

Pain isn't forgiving.

Chapter Thirteen
The Note

How? How is this still in the book? How did he know, know that I would be the one to buy it, not some random shmuck, who had no idea about him, his history? It's almost impossible. It *is* impossible. It seems like something that could only happen in movies, or a book. It makes no sense.

I stare at the paper, frozen in time. The world around me ceases to exist. It's just me and the paper, void around me, spinning in space with no resistance, staring. It addressed me. It was telling me that he loved me, that he'll always be with me. That he wanted me to move on, think of him, but to keep pushing in life. Don't get held back. I know better not to. Don't become cold to the world, not to reject the world around me. It's not healthy. It creates resentment that's too powerful to grow out of. He didn't want me to become like his parents, with cold hearts, always angry with something new, unable to be happy. He wrote that it's not how he raised me, he didn't want his only child to be unhappy, to live miserably, growing alienated from the world around him.

Shaking, tears rolling down my face, mind racing like the Daytona, my heart running at an unhealthy pace. Who do I even tell? My mother isn't all there anymore, and it would destroy her. I couldn't do that to her. Put my mother in that position. I don't have any friends, no wife, no outlets. Kyle knows all that happens, and it's not like I could have a coherent conversation with him, it's a one-way street. I did this to myself, isolating myself these past few months. My first conversation with Shelley couldn't pertain to this, *what do I do?*

***

I decided to sleep it off. No better way to ignore hard feelings than a good shluff. As I open my eyes, I'm no longer in my apartment. I'm in a strange house, one I've never seen before. I look around, searching for answers. The sun shines in through the large windows, beaming sunlight in and illuminating the brown, shaggy carpet. The couches, draped in a plastic cover, look as if they've never been sat in before. Pristine, untouched condition. I begin to walk around, up the stairs, through doors, nothing. As I make my way downstairs, I hear shouting coming from inside the house. I peek around the corner, and see a family of six sitting around the dinner table, partaking in a rather *emotional* conversation. They're yelling about books, the effect it could have in public. They don't seem to notice my presence as I approach them. I try waving my hands in front of them, but no reaction. I don't exist to them. I'm an anomaly. Not real.

They continue their shouting but it begins to become foreign, like Charlie Brown's teacher, nobody making sense other than the son. He looks familiar, but I can't put a name to the face. I go to the fridge to muddle around, I'm hungry, but all I could find are empty containers, stacked in piles of three, as I turn around, the table filled with debris, no one talking, all staring at me. Maybe I shouldn't have gone through their fridge. All their eyes turn white, no pupils, no emotions. I'm confused, but not frightened. The lights dim, a spotlight on the familiar face.

"I'm proud of you, son. You're improving. You found my note, I knew you would. It was just a matter of time. Please, keep taking care of yourself. Call the girl. Be you. Don't be afraid. Things find a way of working out. I know you could make it out of your rut, listen to Kyle, listen to your body, pursue what you love. If I didn't if I listened to my family, I wouldn't have met mom. I wouldn't have had you. My biggest gift to the world wasn't my books, my influence, my way with people, it was you. You have so much to offer, to give. All you have to do is believe in yourself, I always have. Please. For me. We'll see each other again. Until then, be you. Be proud. Be fearless."

Well then. Fuck.

Chapter Fourteen

KkYyLlEe

Po-po-po-po papa Keith showed up it was about time he's been waiting been praying praying for this day to come he talked to him it was real real words real feelings real thoughts we're all so proud of him proud of the growth he's shown and that lady wow that lady was beautiful was smart was perfect for him my time could be done soon I will be glad to leave I love the boy but the boy must move on learn to live without me live as his own person I believe in him we're all proud of him I hope he knows hope he knows he's loved cherished a beautiful boy

He'll know one day,

I'll show him,

For now,

May he rest,

Get some shut eye.

Chapter Fifteen
Am I... Happy?

I don't believe in God, but when I see her, sitting across from me, her eyes hovering above her bags from a short sleep, drinking her coffee and a twinkle across her face, I can't help but believe He put her on this beautiful green Earth. For the first time in a long time, I've felt alive, proud, motivated. I texted her after I found the note, and we went out for a beautiful rooftop dinner, followed by the most romantic arm locking at the top of Mount Royal. I felt at peace, calm. It's been three months since that night, and I don't think I've been so at ease, so comfortable in a while. When I cry about my father, she holds me, Kyle watching, making sure that she doesn't hurt me. I think about her constantly, wishing my father could have met her. He would've loved her. Her sense of humour, her outlook on life, her hatred of things that shouldn't bother her, like a broken headlight. They're so similar like that.

I'm open like a book, I let her read me, see inside my thoughts. That's new for me. I've always been defensive, closed off. Stuck in my thoughts, stubborn and determined to figure things out for myself. I let her help me. Find solutions with me. She's the thunder to my lightning. I'll often wake up in the middle of the night from nightmares, and I'll turn over to her sleeping. So peaceful, so protected. It calms me down, lets me believe everything is okay. Then, Kyle snuggles me to sleep, holding me and keeping me weighed down.

I can be myself with her, let my weirdness out, be my true self and show my interests. Even her flaws are perfect. I'm so happy I went into that bookshop. I don't think I've described myself as *happy* for something in years. Not since the boys were born at least. I miss them. I miss my father. I miss my life, but she helps that a bit. She knows how much her presence helps me benefit, grow.

***

Our first kiss was nothing short of magical. After a fun night of her destroying me at Skee-Ball, I walked her home. As we got to her door, our eyes locked. There's always that feeling when you *know* it's the right time. It's universal, everyone knows the feeling. The sensation that the stars align, that it's time to make the move. I moved in close in the star-lit sky, the wind blowing her hair back like she was in a music video and it was orchestrated perfectly, my hand cupping her razor-sharp jaw, and our lips locked. Fireworks don't come close to describing what was generated. Like the world's prophecy was for us to kiss, the world around us slowed. No one in the universe but us.

The new Big Bang. Atoms colliding generating nuclear forces, a great light glaring, our souls intertwining.

***

There's a psychological theory surrounding colours. How certain colours invoke feelings and represent aspects of life. It's theorized that it plays a major factor in our choices and feelings. She reminds me of the colour blue. I've never been reminded of a colour from someone, the feeling to me is new, my inner love beginning to once again brew. Blue represents belonging, calmness, stability. Strangely, in Latin American cultures, blue signifies mourning. Maybe she's the key. The key to me moving on, finding my own place in this universe.

To find what I can give the universe. The gift my father had seen in me.

Chapter Sixteen
Pages & Plaisir

Pages & Plaisir. Started and ran by Keith Linsar. A quaint bookshop in the Pointe-Claire village of Montreal. It was a beautiful, comfortable building. He never redid the outside, it had the look of an old home, old stones covering the walls, large windows to allow plenty of natural light to fill the space. He set up a reading area by the windows, with worn reclining leather chairs, the type that you sink into when you sit in it. I spent a lot of time there, reading, looking at girls that would walk in. When my dad was in the back, I'd try to flirt with them, which would, more times than not, result in them saying they had a boyfriend or that I was too young for them. You never know unless you shoot your shot! Even Michael Jordan had more missed buckets than makes.

***

Upon arriving in Montreal after meeting my mom in Boston, he had to fill his time somehow. Sure, there was writing, but what would he do during writing blocks, times he needed to get out of the house? With such an adoration for books, he knew he had to be surrounded by them. He would never work in a library, he hated the feel of them and the quietness. He liked the action, interaction, the attention. So, with his earnings, bought an old trinket store that was going out of business. A couple months of renovation later, purchasing of titles and licensing with the government, Pages & Plaisir was up and running.

At first, it wasn't too busy. My dad didn't do any advertising, he held out hope on word of mouth. Luckily, his patience paid its dues. Within six months of opening, the store was packed. Books flying off the shelves, people waiting to sit in the reading area, he even bought a coffee machine to give complimentary coffees to those who bought books. He even got my mom to come in and help, especially when he went into his writing retreats, unable to care for the customers. It was a local favourite. People recommending Keith's bookshop, what a pleasant place to go! Even if you're not interested in books, just going in and enjoying the warmth from the sun, the Linsar's hospitality, was worth it. At some points, he had to keep the shop open past close, even an hour after, because he didn't want to kick people out. Or, he didn't want to wake people up that were enjoying the seats. They looked comfortable, and he had his wife to keep him company. Why would he change anything? It was a win-win.

***

When my mom got pregnant with me, she obviously had to take a step back from helping out. My dad stopped letting people stay past close, so he could go cook my mom dinners, help out around the house. He also had to slow down his writing, as he had no one to help him out at the store, he didn't want to hire anyone. Keep it in the family (and save his pockets, he didn't have to pay anyone). Customers brought in cards, gifts for my parents, congratulations gifts. Mazel Tovs were given, and a notice that my dad would close down shop for a bit after I was born. He wanted to be present, give a helping hand to my mom. Clearly, with the gift giving and all, people were more than understanding. They'd be back the second he opened back up!

A year later, when I had taken my first steps, he announced the grand reopening. For the next couple years, business was as good as ever. But, as life moves on and people change, it got less and less busy. My dad had plenty of time to write, take naps in the chairs, and bring me in to take care of little ol' me. He wasn't upset, happy, he was neutral about it. His royalties were still coming in at full throttle. he was spending time with family, but he spent less time interacting with others. That was life. He came to accept it. He was blessed with a son, plagued by the ever changing world. Radical acceptance. Things were out of his control, would he sit there and weep, damning the world for offsetting his miracle of childbirth? Or would he accept it, be happy with what was going well? Keith, being who he was, chose the latter. Enjoy the uninterrupted time with his kid, show him the world of literature, the portal to another world. Let him explore, be there every step of the way. Cater his world to imagination, creativity.

Let his son have the life he never had. The choices he never had. Let him know, whatever he chose, whenever, he'd always have the undying support of his family.

Chapter Seventeen
The Dilemma of Love

LIFE IS BRIGHTER, TASTES are stronger, motivation is higher, mood is better, and it's all because of her. She found me in the dark, stuck, and shone a light on me. She showed me what life could be like, how the sun could still shine without my father's presence. I think I'm deeply in love. I'm scared though. She told me she loved me the other night and I froze. I didn't know how to respond. I knew my feelings were strong, but was it infatuation, obsession, or love? Kyle came in to save me, gave me the runs, and got her to leave so she didn't get sick. We haven't talked much since. Just the passing text asking how things are.

I'm terrified of moving on, of a new life. We've been seeing each other for close to a year now, it should be time... shouldn't it? Accepting that things are different, that he's gone. I know I feel like this, but I can't transfer the feelings to words. To allow her in. I've been working on it but still a ways to go. I've tried writing it out, time and time again. Searching for the right words, the right way to say it. Draft after draft, nothing working.

I think I'm also afraid to be hurt again. I don't want a repeat of my last marriage, nights at the pub, sleepless nights on the couch, screaming matches and scaring the children. I can't do that again. I know the pain it entails and how it feels to go off the rails. Not what I want, what I need.

***

I decided to ask her to meet me at a coffee shop. A nice, neutral place, where a scene couldn't be made. I didn't want it all to go sideways, feelings going amuck. I got there a half hour early. It gave me enough time to calm down my nerves, slightly. I sat in the chair, foot tapping the ground, eyes glued to the front door, waiting for her to walk in. Heart going a million miles a minute, waiting, waiting, waiting.

Finally, she walked in. Looking beautiful as always, so effortlessly. I could never get enough of it. As she made it to the table, I got up to give her a hug. I broke down instantly. I didn't know how I'd break it to her. How it would go down. The first thing I did, was explain everything. How I was feeling, how much love and adoration I had for her. Tears were welling up in both our eyes. The pain, emotions, were shared. We both felt it. We were one.

And it was time. I told her I had something I needed to do. I saw the sorrow, the pain, regret, appear across her face.

It took me a second to muster up the courage. Would this change everything? Solidify what I've worked on, or break it all down?

I stood up, walked up to her, grabbed her hands, and reached into my pocket. Looked deep into her eyes, and got down on one knee.

Chapter Eighteen
The Journey

ALL ALONE, NO CONTACTS, no destination in mind. This is what I see, watching my father leave his home after his parents found out about his books. I know I'm dreaming, lucid, aware, but fully captivated. I'm watching him, like he's an animal in a zoo, in captivity. Alone in the streets of Oakland, only his notebooks, the clothes on his back and his two feet to stand. With his royalties, there wasn't much holding him back. He could go wherever he'd like to. Oxford, Cambridge, Stanford, the world was his to take. Anywhere he'd go, scholars would be head over heels to take him under their wing. But he didn't want to be under someone, be their student. He was a free mind, couldn't be tied down. He decided to go to the train station, buy the first ticket out of town and manage from there.

***

As he stepped off the train, he was greeted by mist, humidity, and a bustling city. A much different environment from what he was used to. As he explored the city, he was amazed. He had never left Oakland before. The amount of people in another city was crazy! Thousands of more people, minding their own business, with their own lives. Had anyone here read his books? Seen into his creative mind? This all crossed his mind as he approached the Space Needle. Beautiful, rainy Seattle. He decided he didn't mind it there, he could enjoy the quaint humid life. He'd have to buy a winter jacket, endure the cold winters he wasn't familiar with, but he knew he wouldn't be here for long. He'd settle in a warmer climate, surely. He figured he'd write a book here, move to a new city, observe the people, rinse and repeat. He was young, he could be a nomad! He had plenty of time to find the one, settle down. For now, what's the point of settling, when there was a whole world to explore!

Seattle, Nashville, New Orleans, El Paso, Anchorage, Boston. This was the trajectory that young Keith followed. He never wanted to step foot in New York, the hotspot for new talents that it was. Too much competition, too "big city" for him. He bounced from town to town, soaking in the cultures, the people, the history. He was always a sponge for information, he could never get enough. It fueled him, his creative core. He was a red giant in the literary universe, a bigger star than anyone. Not a dying star, just one so powerful no one thought he could continue his tenure, proving the theory wrong every release. His writing was maturing alongside himself. He was a force to be reckoned with.

I watch this, amazed to see the life I never got to experience viewing. The traveling, education and restless nights writing I never knew occurred. He always hid it, or just kept it until I had asked. What could have been if I had just wondered, asked out of curiosity. Everything might have been different.

***

He was in Boston for about three months until he decided to buy a car to get around. He was used to public transport, but felt it was a necessary purchase. He needed alone time, an easier way of observing. His current project, "The Big Bust," took up a lot of space in his mind. Creating a world where the industrial revolution never took place, and it was current times, seeing how different life would be, took a lot of brainpower to imagine. He started to suffer from derealization, he'd get stuck in the world he created, not believing what he saw around him. He was watching himself from the third person, as I was in my dream. Reality started to fade, he couldn't tell the difference between the real world and the book.

He was driving near Northeastern University, stuck in his thoughts. He was on autopilot, just taking where muscle memory allowed. In a last second reflex, he slammed on the breaks. He was about three feet from running someone over. He looked up, and was instantly brought back to reality. There was no abstract, no confusion. Looking at the woman crossing, her hair blowing in the wind, the shock covering her face. He knew then and there.

He found the love of his life.

His life raft.

Chapter Nineteen
A New Life

TO START ANEW IS a beautiful feeling. Leaving the past behind, only the present and future on the map. It's surreal to think I'll be marrying the true love of my life. That my life could turn around, go upwards, as it has, feels like a miracle. I feel real, strong, alive. Ready to take on the world, battle my struggles, move on. She's everything I've ever wanted from life. She gives me purpose, determination. Determination to live life to its fullest, not to be held back. She makes me want to wake up in the morning, get out of bed, take the world on.

Finding love in life is difficult enough, but finding it later on is questionable. Are you just settling? If it's good enough, it should do? But with her, there's no doubt I found my person. Being in her presence makes me smile. It fills my heart. Makes me see the sun rise and makes me proud I did alongside it.

I know my father would be proud, that he'll be there in spirit, watching, smiling. Kyle knows it too. Watching from a distance, I could tell he's proud. Getting ready to pack up and leave. I'll miss him. My shadow puppet, my friend.

Chapter Twenty
Goodbye, for Now

THE CASHIER RINGS ME up for $52.84, and I make my way to the car where Shelley's waiting for me. I buckle up and we start our drive. I haven't been there in forever, and I'm anxious to get there, to see it again. I bought a Moleskine notebook and a ballpoint pen to leave at my father's grave. Give him the tools he held so dearly. When I was clearing out his space, there were piles upon piles of notebooks and empty pen cartridges, I found that reading material had no shortage. I haven't brought myself to read his papers yet, I'm not ready to see his thoughts, ideas, memories. It's an intimate setting I haven't prepared myself for. I still miss him so dearly. I'm going with Shelley, so they could meet each other.

***

When we get there, we each take a rock to his grave. We place it on his headstone and she holds me as I weep. It's difficult to come, to know he's never coming back. To know I'll never have another conversation with him, that the rest of my life will be fatherless. She rubs the headstone and introduces herself. So perfect, so kind. She knows how much this means to me. Shelley knows I want time to myself and my father, so she says it was a pleasure meeting him, and goes to sit in the car.

I sit on the grass next to where he lays, with my head between my knees. Kyle preys closely as I sit here, a long shadow exposing my silhouette along the green grass. The wind blowing through my hair, my tears hitting the ground, my breath shaky. I feel my father close to me, his presence weighing heavy. I tell him about everything. How I met Shelley, that I found his note, that I'm so grateful he's come to my dreams, that he's shown me his life. That he's let me in, with every intention to keep me, his little boy. I tell him how I envision him still here, that he's still in my life. That I'm so appreciative of the time we spent together, the memories we shared, the laughs, the hardships. It all built up a fortress, a stronghold of happiness, strength.

It's hard to bring myself to leave him, to keep pushing forward. I know it's necessary. I'm not who I was months ago. I'm stronger, more resilient. I could do this. One step at a time, one tear to wipe away at a time, it could be done. I'm fighting with a ghost of me, someone I used to be, someone less strong, less able. I need to move forward, grow, stop holding myself back.

Live up to my destiny,

Find my own identity,

And make my father proud.

Chapter Twenty-One

K...

M-M-M-M MY BOY CALLUM he's safe now I've done what I could done what I should I can leave as the sun sets I will disappear into the darkness I've completed my mission my purpose he's set up set up to do wonderful things I can't be more proud proud of what he's accomplished he's always had it inside himself he just needed to see it believe it pursue it I can now rest in peace

And as I leave you Callum,

Just know I will always love you with all my heart and more,

I know our paths will cross again,

Goodbye, Son.

Do Not Stand At My Grave And Weep

'Do not stand at my grave and weep I am not there.

I do not sleep.

I am a thousand winds that blow.

I am the diamond glints on snow.

I am the sunlight on ripened grain.

I am the gentle autumn rain.

When you awaken in the morning's hush

I am the swift uplifting rush

Of quiet birds in circled flight.

I am the soft stars that shine at night.

Do not stand at my grave and cry;

I am not there.

I did not die.'

Mary Elizabeth Frye

About the author

Brendan Rubin is the author of *Heart Burn* and *Grief Hides in the Shadows*. He lives in Montreal with his family.

www.ingramcontent.com/pod-product-compliance
Lightning Source LLC
Chambersburg PA
CBHW061223210726
48294CB00006B/1958